GO HOME FLASH

Illustrations created in pencil and watercolor.

Published by Sourcebooks Jabberwocky, an imprint of Sourcebooks, Inc.
P.O. Box 4410, Naperville, Illinois 60567-4410
(630) 961-3900
Fax: (630) 961-2168
www.jabberwockykids.com

First published by Scholastic New Zealand Limited in 2014.
This edition published under license from Scholastic Australia Pty Limited
on behalf of Scholastic New Zealand Limited.

Library of Congress Cataloging-in-Publication data is on file with the publisher.

Source of Production: Leo Paper, Heshan City, Guangdong Province, China
Date of Production: August 2015
Run Number: 5004260

Printed and bound in China.
LEO 10 9 8 7 6 5 4 3 2 1

GO HOME FLASH

Ruth Paul

sourcebooks
jabberwocky

Time to go!

 Off we go!

Here we go!

Let's go!

Oh no.

Go home, Flash.

Too late. Shut gate.

Sit.

Wait.

Mean gate.

GRRRR!

Jump gate!

Go home, Flash.

Small hole.

Dig hole.

Big hole.

Down hole...

Up.

Shake.

Stroll.

Go home, Flash.

Sniff smell,

find smell,

good smell,

strong smell!

Uh-oh...
wrong smell?

Go home, Flash.

Yay, shops!

Love shops.

Food shops...
meat chops!

Car stops.

Go home, Flash.

Can't play.

Not today.

Don't stray.

Sit.

STAY.

Sneak away.

FLASH!

Where is Flash?

Running free...

cat...

tree...

scratch flea.

Come on, Flash.